Cosmic Collection #1

Don DeBon

Cosmic Collection #1

Don DeBon

First Printing
Copyright © 2019, 2020, 2022 Don DeBon

ISBN 978-1-948819-12-1
ISBN 978-1-948819-08-4 **(e-book)**

Contents

Donnie and the Fly

Donnie dragged his feet across the wooden floor, making swishing sounds as he shuffled into his grandfather's study. On the wall, his grandfather had mounted several large fish. Donnie remembered they were called bass, or something like that.

He walked over to his Grandfather seated at his desk looking through a magnifier as he placed another feather on a long metal shank and wrapped thread around it several times. "Whatcha doing Poppy?"

He had always called him Poppy. He didn't know why, but as long as he could remember, he was Poppy.

"Tying a fly," Poppy said.

"A fly? I didn't know you could make those! But it doesn't look anything like a fly I squished yesterday. Sorry if it was yours."

Poppy laughed. "No no, not that kind of fly. The kind you catch fish with."

Donnie mouthed the words. "Catch fish with it? But it doesn't look anything like a worm!"

"Fish do bite on things other than worms, Donnie," Poppy chuckled.

Donnie's eyes went wide. "They do?"

Poppy nodded. "They do indeed. This is a fishing fly and you use it with a fly rod." He pointed to a rod in the corner in its fabric travel case with the reel still clearly visible at the bottom.

Donnie walked over to the rod. "Fly rod? I don't see wings on it. What makes it a fly rod?"

Poppy smiled. "The way it is made. You see, fly fishing is an art. It takes a special rod to do it." He grabbed a tuft of hair and began winding a long thread around, attaching it to the metal.

Donnie came back over to his Poppy's desk. "When will the fly be done?" He watched Poppy dip a pin into a bottle and dripped a strong smelling clear liquid on one end of the fly.

"It is now. Well, once it dries." He sat back in his chair and lifted Donnie up into his lap, so he could get a better look.

Donnie looked over the metal contraption with smooth steel jaws that sat clamped to the closest corner of the desk. It gripped the bottom of the fly. "Wow."

"I hope that fish in the ol' creek thinks so too! I've been trying to get him for six years now."

* * *

The next day Donnie came into Poppy's looking for that new fly. He climbed into Poppy's old leather desk chair. The fly was still there in that metal thing.

He sighed.

Poppy couldn't go fishing today. Even though it is Saturday, a neighbor needed help moving some big thing. A fridge, he thought he heard Grandma say. And Poppy was never one to say no to a friend in need.

He sat back in the oversized chair and dangled his feet as he looked at the fly. I was so pretty the fish couldn't help but bite on it. "That's it!" he muttered. "I'll take the fly and catch that ol' fish for Poppy! Won't he be surprised!"

Donnie sat forward, looking at the fly. He pulled at it a little, but the jaws held on tight. He stood up on the chair seat and looked at the thing holding the fly all over. On the back, another piece of flat metal stood pointing down. He remembered once how Poppy pulled something like that to open something else. "Could it be that?" He reached out and pulled at the metal bar. It stood firm. He tried rocking it back and forth and the fly rotated in the jaws but didn't come loose.

He thought he heard something and looked up. When he did, his hand came back and out, flipping the metal bar up. The jaws released and the fly fell onto the desk.

Hearing it fall, he thought it might have been ruined. Then he realized the jaws had released it unharmed.

Donnie carefully reached forward and picked up the fly. It felt so light. He smiled, dropped it in a little box Poppy had left on the edge of his desk, picked up the box, grabbed Poppy's fly rod, and headed out the door.

* * *

Grandma was in the kitchen making something. He heard that big mixing thing that she used to make bread or cookies. Grandma watched as it whirled through the batter. Donnie always loved helping her clean the metal beaters. They tasted sooo good. He watched her stop the machine it as she added an egg. He waited until she started the motor again before he slipped past her and out the kitchen door.

Donnie skipped his way down the winding path behind

Poppy's house, past the pump house, and towards the creek, humming as he went. It took him twenty minutes on his short little legs, but he didn't slow until he reached the rocks.

The creek's level had dropped considerably during the hot summer. Revealing a lot more rocks than Donnie remembered a few weeks ago.

Donnie stumbled down the creek bed. Rocks stuck out at every angle possible, and he had to go slow so he didn't fall. There were rocks bigger than Poppy's truck, to small rocks he could put in his pocket. And everything in between. Holding the fly rod and the box, he almost fell several times as the jagged rocks reached out to grab his feet.

After a while, he reached the area in the creek where the further bank held a deep and slow pool. Poppy told him big fish like to stay there. He hoped the fish listened to him today. A strong breeze whipped through the evergreens high on the hill above the creek, causing the smell of pine to waft down.

Donnie set the case down on the ground and unzipped it, revealing the rod. It was in two pieces, but he knew how to put them together. His pole worked the same way. He slid the top part of the rod into the small waiting hole in the base of the other. Put together, the rod was a lot longer than he realized. It must have been even taller that Poppy!

The line was different from what he was expecting. Only the very end was clear, the rest was bright orange and thick. He threaded the line through the rod second part of the rod and smiled. But his smile quickly faded when he didn't see a way to attach the fly. There wasn't a little metal clip on the end like he was used to. "How do you put it on? There must be a way."

He looked at it again, and he remembered Poppy showing him how to tie a new metal clip on his line when the old one broke. "Maybe that is how?"

He took the fly and threaded the clear part of the line through the little eye of the fly. Then he folded the line in on itself, through the eye again and around the loop over the hook, tying it off like he did his shoes. He pulled it tight and tugged at the fly. The knot held fast. "It worked!"

Donnie stood back up and moved a little closer to the water. The smell of wet mossy rocks filled his nostrils. He pulled at the fly, causing the reel to click as it released the line. He tossed the bunched up line into the water. The thick line floated like a big cancerous blob. "That's not going to work," he muttered. "I know Poppy said this isn't as easy as my rod, but there must be a way."

He looked up at the tall rod. Being much longer, maybe he could use it to whip the line out to where the fish is. Donnie held his arm up high, pulled the rod straight up and started whipping the line around. He gave the rod a firm quick move forward, hoping the line would go out into the deep water.

With a loud *crack*, the line flew out into the water.

Donnie's eyes went wide. At first he thought he had broken Poppy's rod, but it looked okay. So did the reel. So what made that sound? He decided he had to pull in the line and check the fly. He looked at the reel again, but it wasn't anything like his. Nothing to crank on. Only a little lever. He pressed it and the center of the reel started to turn, very slowly. It clicked as it turned, pulling in the wad of line he had taken out earlier. The reel continued clicking, but when all the line had returned, horror hit him in the pit of his stomach.

There, on the end of the line, the fly remained attached, but it was not the same. All the feathers were missing, as were most of the hair. A long strand of red thread had come undone and stood waving in the breeze. The only thing left besides the hook and the red string was a tiny bit of fuzz stubbornly remained. Held by the clear stuff Poppy had put on.

"Oh no! I have ruined it! What am I going to do?" Donnie sunk down, sitting on the dry creek bed. Uneven sharp rocks poked at his bottom, but he didn't even notice. "I have ruined Poppy's precious fly! Now he will never catch that fish!"

He thought about heading up to Poppy's house right then. But it had taken him quite a while to get here. "Might as well try as long as I'm here. At least I can't hurt it anymore."

Donnie stood back up, pulled out more line and whipped the fly around several times, and this time moved a little slower when he moved the rod forward. The line flipped out into the water, but he didn't hear a crack this time. The water took the fly downstream and into the deep area. He waited, but nothing happened. "Didn't think any fish was dumb enough to bite on a broken fly!"

Suddenly he felt something. His eyes went wide as the line gave a firm tug. He yanked hard on the rod, pulling it back like Poppy had shown him with his own rod when a fish bit a worm. The end of line thrashed. He *did* have a bite! He wondered how to pull in the fish. The reel was too slow to pull in a fish. The fish pulled *hard,* jerking the rod down. It was also too strong. Donnie decided to just force the fish out of the water. He pulled and took a step backwards. The fish fought back, and the reel let out a little line.

Donnie's eyes went wide, and he slapped his hand over the reel. "You're not letting out anymore line you dumb reel!" He yanked hard trying to take back the extra line the fish had taken.

The fish thrashed in the deep pool. Donnie pulled harder and took a step back, but the fish fought even stronger and a little more line slipped from the reel. After several minutes, Donnie's arms were starting to get tired of holding the rod up so high while taking backward steps, but he wasn't about to give up.

Then the edge of his toe caught on the side of a large uneven rock, and he went down. The line grated on a sharp rock at the edge of the pool, snapping it instantly.

The fly rod went up straight, shooting the rest of the line over Donnie's head. He stood up, rubbing his foot and shin where he had hit. "Darn fish!" he muttered and shook his fist. "I'll get you!" He hit the little lever on the reel and the line started to click in. But when all the thick line sat safely in the reel, nothing was on the end of it.

The fly was gone.

Donnie stood there looking at the missing end. Not much of the clear part of the line was left. And the part that was, looked frazzled. He hung his head and sat down on the sharp rocks again, putting the rod carefully on one of the bigger rocks. "Now I didn't only break it, but I lost it too!" he wailed. Tears ran down his cheeks as he thought about how to tell Poppy.

His throat felt like it had a boulder in it, but there was nothing he could do. He picked up the fly rod, stumbled his way over to the case, split the rod in two, slipped both pieces into the case, and zipped it closed. He picked up the case and made his way back to Poppy's house.

His grandmother spotted him this time as he stepped through the kitchen door. "Donnie! I thought you were upstairs! Where have you been? And have you been crying?" She saw the case in his hand. "What are you doing with Poppy's rod?"

Donnie hung his head. "Grandma, I ... I ... I messed up."

His grandmother bent down on her haunches and looked into his eyes. "Honey, what did you do?"

"I …I …I can't tell you!" He ran upstairs to his room, slamming the door shut.

He slid Poppy's case under his bed. He lay on the bed, burying his face into one of the large pillows. Tears creating two hot paths soaked into the pillow as he cried.

Over an hour later, Donnie heard a knock at his door. He sat up in time to see Poppy open the door and step inside. "Donnie? Want to tell me what happened?"

Donnie buried his face back into the pillow. "I …I …can't!"

Poppy walked over to Donnie's bed and sat on it, placing his strong hand on Donnie's shoulder. "Try."

Donnie sat up, his eyes red. "I …I took your special fly and tried to catch the fish. But I broke it and then I lost it when the fish snapped the line! Poppy, I'm sooo sorry. Please don't hate me."

Poppy blinked. "Hate you? Why in the world would you think I would hate you? I could *never* hate you. You are my grandson and I love you. That will never change no matter what."

Donnie rubbed his nose and let out a sniffle. "Really? Even after I took your special fly?"

Poppy nodded. "Of course. And I can make another. Just don't ever take anything of mine without asking again, okay?"

Donnie sniffled again. "Okay. Poppy, I'm really sorry."

Poppy smiled. "I know you are. Let's forget it, okay? Tell you what, you said the fish bit on the fly after you broke it?"

Donnie rubbed his hand under his nose again. "Uh-huh."

"Well then, how about you show me what it looked like?

Perhaps we can make one just like it and the fish will bite again."

The tear-soaked corners of Donnie's mouth started to turn up. "I can do that."

"I thought you might." Poppy stood up, gathered Donnie into his arms, took a step, and set him back down with his feet on the floor. "Come on." He held out his hand.

Donnie smiled. "Okay, Poppy." He placed his hand in Poppy's as they went downstairs to make an ever better fly.

The Dragon Princess

Cassie sat on the couch in her old sweat pants, shirt, and hair pulled back in a ponytail watching an old movie on the classic movie channel. She had hoped John would ask her out tonight, but apparently he was busy. Next to her Jenny, a nine-pound white Japanese Chin except for light brown and tan coloring on her head with a little white strip from that went her nose to the back of her head, and a few brown patches on her hindquarters, lay stretched out sound asleep. She was one, if not *the* most beautiful dog Cassie ever had.

"Just you and me tonight girl, I'm glad I can always count on you." The little dog didn't stir, and she heard slight snores emanating from the animal. Jenny had come into her life four years ago after her previous dog, Buster had died suddenly. Cassie couldn't deal with the hole he had left in her life, and she ran right out and got Jenny.

Cassie had planned on a bigger dog but then realized in her tiny apartment, another miniature-sized companion would be best. Looking at all the dogs through the glass wall in the pet store, only one looked back at her. No matter where Cassie moved, this little fluff ball watched her. "Jenny really likes you," one of the caretakers said.

"Oh?"

The girl nodded. "Mm-hmm. She normally doesn't watch other people, or even notice them unless we bring her to them."

Cassie cocked her head again, looking at the little dog. "Jenny is her name?"

"Well, it is what we have called her, and she seems to respond to it," the girl shrugged.

"Can I see her?"

"Of course." The girl went behind the glass wall and picked the little dog from her cage and brought her out. "Would you like to see her in one of our inspection rooms?"

"No, I would just like to hold her first if I may?"

She nodded. "Certainly." She placed the little dog in the crook of Cassie's arm. "I need to check something up front. I will be right back."

Once in her arms, Cassie knew Jenny would come home with her. The little dog seemed to smile and her big eyes glowed with a feeling of 'take me home' and Cassie was happy to oblige.

Jenny was almost full-grown at the time, and it surprised Cassie someone hadn't taken this little fluff ball home long before. But it worked out, and it seemed the animal was made for her. They did almost everything together, unless she went on dates, or to a location that didn't allow dogs. But Jenny didn't feel or act like a dog. Or at least like any dog she had before. She was already house-trained and never went inside at all. She hated anything dirty, to the point if her bed had hair or dirt on it she would give a more forceful snort, and glare until it was cleaned.

And oh, that snort was the most expressional one Cassie had ever heard. It was almost as if Jenny was talking to her. It didn't sound like a pig, more like a delicate little quick breath through her tiny nose. Not near a sneeze, but a lot more than a normal breath. Between the varying snorts, a certain flick of her tail, and a look with those big eyes, Cassie always knew what she wanted. Almost as if she spoke to her. While most dogs would bark, Jenny never did unless someone was banging on the door. Another reason she fit in so well; you never wanted your neighbors complaining about your dog's barking. Especially in an apartment with strict rules. But even when Jenny chose to raise her voice, it was the cutest little sound. Nothing like other dog's siren blast that felt like needles through your ears.

Jenny never pulled on the leash, instead walking alongside Cassie in perfect synchronicity. Cassie often wondered who could have trained this dog so well yet let her go to a pet store? It didn't make any sense.

* * *

Cassie's mind snapped back to the present with a faint knock at her door. She got up in slow motion as not to disturb the little dog at her side and looked through the peep-hole in the door. A delivery man stood outside holding a flat box. She pushed the button next to the door, toggling the intercom. "Yes?"

"I have your pizza here. You wanna open up?"

The hairs on Cassie's neck stood up. She hadn't ordered a pizza. And her wheat and milk allergies wouldn't let her eat it even if she had. She pushed button again. "You have the wrong apartment. I can't eat pizza."

"Look Miss, this is the address they gave me."

Cassie sighed, loosing patience. *Why do men never listen?* "I don't care, it is a mistake."

"I know I have it right. Fine, would you at least sign this to show I *tried* to deliver it and was here? Otherwise, it is coming out of my pocket." He held up a thin slip of paper.

Cassie shook her head. She knew some companies were making it hard on their employees, but this was ridiculous. "Very well, slide it under the door and I will."

"Are you kidding me? Look, I'm not armed or anything," he spun around holding his black jacket wide open, "I'm just a pizza guy."

Cassie rolled her eyes. *Sheesh! Some people!* She flipped open two dead bolts, turned the knob, and pulled the door open. The man was smiling, and she didn't see the box anymore. She was about to ask where is the slip when he raised a hand. He said something incoherent and a blue ball of light flew out of his palm and rammed into Cassie, hurling her back against the wall behind the door. She couldn't move. Something held her pinned, but she didn't see anything. The man took three steps, closing the gap between them entering the apartment.

"Now, I am only going to ask this once. Where is the Princess?"

Cassie blinked. "The who?"

"The Princess! Don't deny it. I can see the residue from her life force all over this place. I won't ask again. Where is she!"

Cassie tried to shake her head, but the invisible force held her fast. "I told you I don't know what–"

You will not harm her. Stop now if you know what is good for you. A female voice boomed from everywhere.

The man turned to see Jenny on the floor looking up at him. Her fur ruffled and her lantern eyes narrowed into slits. A tiny gap in her lips displayed tiny needle teeth. Cassie had never seen the dog like this. She was normally a little angel, well unless she tried to trim her toenails. But she looked even more threatening now. "Well ... well. I never would have guessed, why did you–"

Jenny's eyes narrowed further and light blue bolts of energy racked the man's body. He shook violently and fell to the ground unconscious. Another man burst through the door. Jenny whipped her head to the right, and the man froze in mid-step, blue electric arcs raging up and down his body before he too fell into a heap.

I am sorry for this. I never thought they would find me here. I thought I had blocked all traces. She sat down and cocked her head. The force holding Cassie released. *Please forgive me.*

Cassie took a step forward. "Jenny? Is that you? Or am I totally freaking out here? Well, of course I'm freaking out. Or asleep. Dogs don't talk." Although she didn't see the dog's mouth move. It was as if Cassie heard it in her head.

We do if we aren't really a dog. She turned her head towards the door, blinked, the door shut, and both deadbolts flipped. *That won't stop them for long when more arrive, and more powerful now that they know where I am. Thankfully they far underestimated my abilities. These two will be out for almost a day. More than enough time for us to get far away from here.*

Cassie shook herself and pinched her right arm. *Ow!* "Okay, I'm not dreaming."

No, you are not.

Cassie looked into Jenny's eyes. "How are you doing this? What are you?"

Cassie felt a sigh in her mind. *Magic, my dear. I thought you would have figured that out by now.*

"What are you?"

Jenny's body began to glow. An orb of pure white light grew from her center, growing until it enveloped her entire body. Cassie stood there blinking in the harsh light for several seconds until the orb began to shrink. When it disappeared Jenny's body had lengthened and narrowed to an almost serpentine shape, but kept the same original size over all. Her head and teeth had grown, and iridescent scales covered her body. Most were green with a narrow golden stripe down her back and sides. "I am Princess Amayah Oohira."

Cassie blinked. "You are a dragon?"

"Yes. My parents have ruled my kind for centuries."

"And why were you masquerading as a dog?"

Amayah smiled. "I thought that would be obvious. A walking, talking dragon in your world? I would have drawn a lot of attention, and I was trying to hide. Not be seen."

"Why?"

"I grew tired of being a princess and our realm. I found yours much more interesting."

"And who are these guys?"

"Members of the Black Dragons. They have been trying to depose my Father for over a hundred years. I thought I had masked any method they could use to track me, and I failed. As I said before, we need to leave. More will come."

"Why do they want you? To force your Father to give up his throne?"

Amayah nodded. "Yes, in essence. However, because they are here now, it can only mean my Father must be in ill health."

"Why?"

"Because I doubt they would have attempted this otherwise. My Father's wrath is legendary. Please, we must go now."

Cassie shook her head once again to make sure she wasn't hallucinating. "All right, let me get a few things together."

"You don't need them. I can form whatever you need," Amayah said.

"Oh? Well, I still would like to have my own pajamas if you don't mind. Besides, if we don't have any luggage, people are going to look at us weird."

Amayah sighed. "Very well, but please hurry."

Cassie moved to the bedroom with Amayah following behind as she took down a suitcase from the top shelf of the closet and started pulling clothing out of her dresser drawers and placing them in the case. She packed several pairs of underwear, pajamas, pants, shirts, and even a couple of dresses. After she closed the suitcase, she pulled out a pair of black dress pants, cream blouse, and quickly changed into them. "You never did tell me where are going."

"Japan, the portal to my realm is there."

Cassie laughed. "Now why didn't I guess that."

Amayah cocked her head. "I don't understand."

"Never mind," Cassie said, closing the case. "And I think you had better look like a dog again, unless you don't care to attract a lot of attention now."

Amayah smiled. "I have a better idea." She began to glow again and the white orb of energy grew from her middle enveloping her as before. But this time it expanded several times its previous size until it was almost the same size as Cassie. When it began to shrink a new form stood before her. An Asian woman Cassie's age with long black hair that reached past her shoulders. She wore a business suit with a black jacket, white blouse, black skirt, and matching three inch high heels. Amayah smiled again. "I think this will let me go anywhere, compared to a dog form."

Cassie blinked. "You can become human?"

"Of course.   It is fairly simple shape-shifting magic. Although it still takes some time to master."

"Wow, okay, but I guess I had better put on better clothes," Cassie smiled, "I forgot you are a princess. Then I will call and get us a flight." Cassie pulled a skirt out of her closet and slipped out of her slacks.

Amayah blinked. "A flight? What for?"

"How else are we going to get to Japan?"

Amayah laughed.   "You humans, always forgetting the simplest things. You do remember I can do magic, yes?"

Cassie blushed when she realized she had forgotten. "Well …yes …of course." She slipped into the skirt and pulled up the zipper.

"Even without magic I can tell you didn't. But that is fine. I will not take it as lying to me, but embarrassment."

Cassie blushed even more and mumbled "Thank you." She sat on her bed and slipped on a pair of two inch black pumps. "And how are we going to get there?"

"By portal, of course.   I can create portals to take us anywhere on this planet. However, I can't land us near our destination without raising the alarm.   In fact, the further away our landing point is, the better."

Cassie stood up. "I see. And should I now call you A-mo-ah?"

Amayah laughed. "No, it would be best if you keep calling me Jenny in public. While I am certain you would learn to pronounce my name properly, I do not wish to call undue attention to us."

Cassie smiled. "Good idea." She picked up her suitcase. "Ready when you are."

Just then she heard something slam into her apartment

door. She looked out of the bedroom to see a shimmering wall of color covering the door and the wall it attached to. "Good, because their reinforcements have arrived." Amayah pointed to the shimmering energy wall. "That will hold them for a few minutes, but no more." She raised a finger and started muttering something Cassie couldn't quite figure out. Amayah's fingertip started glowing, and she held it out in front of herself for a few moments, then started moving it in a large clockwise circle. As she did it left a red line of energy in the air. Amayah kept moving and a few seconds later the two ends met. The red human-sized circle's glow intensified. A bright flash emanated from it and the center now showed another location. Cassie saw a road and several signs in Japanese. It was almost like a scene from the travel channel. "Go! Now!"

There was another loud noise from the door, and this time the energy barrier shattered. Another hit and the door splintered. Cassie didn't have to be told twice she jumped into the portal with Amayah right behind her.

The door split in two, with one half swiveling away on its strained hinges and the other half falling inward. Several men wearing all black with a matching jacket sporting the image of a coiled dragon on the shoulders burst into the room. But the portal had already started to shrink and before they could get within two steps of it, it reduced to a point and disappeared.

* * *

In front of a large cherry tree, an orange-red orb flashed from a point, exploding out into a human-sized oval. Cassie emerged from the swirling magic ring with Amayah right behind her. The portal fluctuated, flashed, collapsed to a dot, and disappeared.

Cassie looked around. They were at the entrance to a park of some kind. Worn slides, benches that needed a coat of paint, and several monkey bars stood near them. She could see stores and the street a short distance away. The short, narrow buildings only two stories tall differed from any other city she had been to before; but the sign containing a drawing of a dog and several words in Japanese clinched it. She was in Japan all right. Cassie gripped the case in her hand tighter and let out a very audible breath.

Amayah turned. "What is the problem?"

Cassie smiled and shifted from one high-heeled foot to another. "Nothing, I'm just glad no one saw us appear from nowhere."

One corner of Amayah's mouth tilted skyward. "That would not have been a problem, I could make them forget if needed."

Cassie stifled a giggle. "And when wouldn't that be a problem? I mean, we don't just see people pop out of nowhere."

Amayah's smile broadened. "Perhaps, but you humans tend to quickly forget something not normal to you. Assuming you must have been seeing things. If you recall, you pinched yourself several times when you found out my true identity."

Cassie nodded. The warm wind blew and flipped her hair back. "You have a point." Amayah began walking towards the park entrance, and the street beyond it. "Where are we going again?"

"Where the portal to my realm is, of course."

"It's in a park?"

Amayah laughed. "No, of course not. I didn't want to arrive right next to it. The Black Dragons might expect that. But I am sure they won't be watching from this direction, or that I would take a typical human route there."

"Where is it then?" Cassie followed Amayah out of the park and onto the street. She could see a few people in the nearby stores and other businesses, but the area was remarkably vacant otherwise. Being the middle of the day, she assumed there would be many people on the street and several cars going by. But apparently this area was not busy.

Amayah turned with a gleam in her eye. "In a place you call Ryoan-ji Temple."

"It's in a temple? How are we going to get there? Or even get in? You said you wanted to use human methods?"

"That is true, and with many temples that might have been a problem, however, this one allows many tourists on a regular basis." She turned and began walking up the street.

"And how far away is it?"

"A few of your miles."

Cassie blinked. "Miles? Are you kidding? I'm not walking miles in these heels! Why didn't you tell me! I would have worn sneakers!"

"I didn't tell you to mirror my dress."

"I know that, but I felt with you being a princess and all, I should dress up a little. Can you at least change my shoes into flats?"

Amayah nodded, pinching her lips together. "I can, but I have a better idea. I'm just looking for the proper place."

Cassie followed along behind her, looking up and down the street, and crossed the electric train tracks. "Looking for what?"

"Here."

Cassie looked around. On the left side she saw several closed businesses, and on the right a nearly empty parking lot. "What? There is nothing here."

Amayah grinned, taking two quick steps approaching an empty parking space. "Exactly." She closed her eyes and her palm raised as she uttered something Cassie couldn't quite hear. A ball of light flashed from her palm, into the vacant space in front of her, expanded, flickered, flashed, and disappeared leaving behind a two door black car with sleek lines, a red line along each large air intakes on either side that ran down the full length of the car, and clear crest shaped logo with a stallion stood out in the middle on the hood.

* * *

Cassie stood there blinking for a minute until she realized her mouth had dropped open, and she closed it. "A Porsche?"

"Yes. Shall we go?" Amayah walked to the passenger side, popped open the door, turned, slid into the seat, swung her legs in, and shut the door. "Well?"

Cassie blinked several more times and nodded. She moved towards the driver's door, pulled it open, threw her bag into the little space behind Amayah's seat, she slid into the seat, swung her legs in –the cool fabric brushing against her leg as she did so–, and closed the door. Her long fingers gripped the smooth leather-covered steering wheel. Her head tilted as she leaned back in total bliss, reveling in her dreams of wanting a car like this, but never thought she would.

Cassie's eyes snapped open to see Amayah dangling a key in front of her nose. An attached keyring, imprinted with the Porsche crest, wiggled back and forth in sync with the motion. The corner of Amayah's mouth twitched up. "I think you might need this."

Warmth radiated throughout Cassie's body as she giggled. "Yeah, I might." She took the key with her right hand, feeling the back of the leather fob slide along her middle finger as she did so. She went to put the key in the ignition and laughed, remembering Porsche's had them on the left side. She dropped the key into her left hand and placed it into the ignition slot on the dash. With a turn, the engine roared to life, startling her and the throaty bellow out of the back sent a chill up her spine. Cassie had never driven a car with such power before. Most of the time, her car back home was reliable, but once and while you jammed down the gas peddle and it just said 'what?' for several seconds before it leapt into action.

She gripped the steering wheel tighter and turned to Amayah with a twinkle in her eye.

Amayah smiled as a quick breath came out of her nose in a tiny *heh*. "I know you always wanted one. Now shall we go?"

Cassie looked at her. "To where?"

"Why to Ryoan-ji temple and the portal, of course."

Cassie chuckled. "Of course, I knew that part, but you will have to guide me."

"That's a given." Amayah pointed to the street heading north. "That way."

Cassie nodded as she put the car in gear, thankful her Father had taught her how to drive a stick-shift on his old truck. She flipped on the left turning signal, then switched it to the right, as they turned out of the parking lot and headed north.

There was no one else on the street making it easier for her to get the feel of driving on a different side of the road. Once in a while a pedestrian would cross the street, which she had to slow down for, but otherwise they were vacant. Not what she expected in Japan. Cassie always had the impression of a large city's traffic being heavily congested, no matter what country. But obviously, in this area of Japan, the traffic was less at this time of day, even being a city.

After several minutes of travel, with Amayah pointing up this street or down that one. Cassie noticed a black van several car lengths behind them. She didn't know why, but it sent a cold chill up her spine. "Amayah? Umm, could the Black Dragons be following us?"

Amayah gave a dismissive wave. "I suppose it is possible to track the portal to where we were, but we moved away from there quickly. Even if they arrived, they shouldn't be able to track us. I put several additional protections on us before we arrived."

"Well, could you take a look behind us? I keep seeing this black van. It has followed us after several turns. They aren't getting any closer, but I keep seeing them."

Amayah turned to peek out the rear window. Sure enough, she saw a black van some distance away which followed them after yet another turn. "Oh dear." She squinted and her eyes flashed. "Yes, I can see them. They are Black Dragons."

Cassie's knuckles went white as she gripped the steering wheel tighter and her palms began to sweat. "What do we do?"

Amayah sat back in her seat. "We lose them of course."

Cassie looked over for a second and back. "You're kidding?"

Amayah grinned, her eyes gleaming. "Not at all. You have the car. Take advantage of it. This vehicle is far more substantial than theirs. You shouldn't have any trouble in doing so."

Cassie forced out a breath. "First time I'm in Japan and I'm going to break every traffic law there is." She sighed again and wrung her hands around steering wheel several times. She knew she might be able to do as Amayah had asked. While she had never tried it, on several simulators her old boyfriend used to say she had an uncanny ability for driving and beat him every time on every driving game he had. And he had a lot of them. She blew out another breath. Her hand reached down for the gear selector and stopped, her palm rested upon it as her other foot reached for the clutch. "Hang on!"

She hit the clutch, jammed the car into a lower gear, and shoved the accelerator half-way to the floor. The car leapt forward in a sequel of burning tires, leaving smoke and black streaks on the road as it did. The black van, having realized they had been spotted, gave away all pretense of stealth and gunned their engine, causing their tires to sequel in return.

The gap between them started to close. Cassie pushed down the accelerator further, trying to maintain or increase that buffer. They went faster and faster. Squealing around this corner, then another. Thankful no one had got in their way, although Cassie did blow past a few cars by switching lanes very quickly.

She never thought she would be in an urban drag race.

Cassie slid around another corner and would have hit a pedestrian if it wasn't for Amayah flicking her hand, creating an orb of blue shards of light to flash into being around the person and push them out of the way.

Cassie smiled, knowing what Amayah had done. and she pushed the accelerator down a little further. She slammed the clutch in and switched into the highest gear for a few seconds before she had to jam on the breaks to make the next corner. She slid into the other lane and almost hit a tiny Mazda if it wasn't for Amayah waving them out of the way and onto the vacant sidewalk.

The black van almost tipped over on the last corner, but seeing a flash of colored light on the tires told Cassie why they didn't. Magic, had to be.

Cassie narrowed her eyes, wondering what to do. They could get away in a straight out race. But in the middle of a city she had to keep slowing down to make corners, or not kill someone. "What should we do? The normal methods aren't getting us very far. I'm doing my best, but we aren't getting away from them."

"Yes I know, they're cheating."

Cassie's right eyebrow went up. "Cheating?"

"Yes, they are using their magic outright. While I did on that one pedestrian and the car. It was to prevent a collision. They are using it to keep up with us. And they shouldn't be. They are more desperate than I thought they were."

"What do we do?"

Amayah blew out a breath. "I don't know. Could you try going somewhere else?"

Cassie's eyes went wide. "I don't know this city, let alone the country! You know it, I don't!"

"Good point. Take the next road to the right. We might have a chance."

Cassie gripped the shifter in her right hand and put her foot on the clutch, ready to take the next turn as fast as she could. "Where are we going?"

"You will know when we get there."

Cassie's eyes went wide and her tongue dove into a corner of her cheek as the Porsche squealed around the corner. The black van did the same, but by this time they had turned again into an alley and Amayah told her to stop and wait.

She wondered how this was going to work, but she did as Amayah asked.

Three seconds later, the black van roared past. Cassie pointed her eyes wide and Amayah relaxed a little as she leaned back in her seat. "Apparently they aren't cheating entirely, or they would have seen us. But I would suggest we get going again before they realize they are on the wrong track and head back."

"You don't have to tell me twice." Cassie jammed her foot on the pedal, racing out of the alleyway and back on to the street, heading in the opposite direction of the van.

Amayah directed to turn left, right, then left again, racing down several streets. "I'm not seeing them, are you?"

Cassie shook her head. "Nope, I haven't seen them since the alleyway."

"Good, I think we lost them."

Cassie, relieved, let her foot relax and the accelerator came back up. They urged forward in their seats from the deceleration as the engine's roar reduced to a mere purr.

Amayah directed up two more streets and over. By this time, the buildings had become less congested. And in the area beyond on the right had far more grass and trees then she had seen since they had arrived. On the left still held buildings and the city they had been racing through.

After two miles, Amayah pointed. "It is over here on the right."

Cassie turned her head. "What is?"

"The Ryoan-ji temple."

"Seriously? Are you kidding me? It is really in the Ryoan-ji temple? I thought you meant nearby."

"Yes, I told you that is where the portal to my realm is located."

"I know that, but even I know the Ryoan-ji temple. It has the most famous rock garden in Japan!"

Amayah turned. "So you *do* know Japan!"

Cassie smirked. "Well, *that* I do anyway."

They turned into the temple's parking lot. When they got out, a Japanese man inside the toll booth at the other end smiled at them pointing the sign that told the current prices. Cassie leaned over. "I don't have any money, at least not Japanese Yen."

Amayah put her hand behind her back, closed her eyes for a second, muttering something. When her hand returned, she placed several folded-over bills in Cassie's hand. "That should be sufficient."

Cassie blinked, counting out the bills. There was a lot more here than what they needed. "I would say so." She walked over to the booth, taking out one of the smaller bills, handing it to the man. He smiled and gave her change while saying something in Japanese. She just smiled back and inclined her head a little as he placed the coins in her hand. Walking away, she leaned close to Amayah. "What did he say? I think it was 'thank you'."

Amayah tilted her head to the right as one eye narrowed. "Something like that. More along the lines of wishing us an enjoyable time."

"I figured that much," Cassie said.

Amayah smiled. "And you say you don't know Japan."

"Well, I told you I have heard a *few* things."

They walked up the stone steps leading up along the path. The path twisted, branching off into several directions. They stuck with the one leading up to the main temple building. They passed a large pond and several smaller buildings until they reached the main temple itself. Walking close to the buildings, Cassie never thought she would be this close to Japanese architecture. And it was certainly more different from she even expected, and even more so considering how old this building was and the history it had seen unaccosted by anyone or anything especially, considering all the tourists coming through.

But then she realized the Japanese have more respect of property and heritage in their culture. That, and she assumed there was more security here than what she was seeing to guard the precious buildings.

As they approached, a sign posted in English and Japanese told them to remove their shoes. Cassie kicked off her heels off to the side of a pile of footwear and felt the relief in her calves. They were her best pair, but she knew if someone stole them, Amayah would replace them. Perhaps with an even better set.

Amayah carefully removed her heels and set them down next to Cassie's, revealing the detailed pedicure topped with blue polish visible through her nylon clad feet on the wooden step.

They turned and walked along the hallway passing several barefoot tourists until they reached the rock garden. Amayah began to take a step closer but Cassie leaned over before she could. "Are you saying it is *in* the rock garden itself?"

Amayah grinned. "Yes, why wouldn't it be?"

"How are you going to use it with all these people around?"

The corners of Amayah's mouth turned up further as her grin widened. "This small of a group I can handle." He held out her hand, smiled, and pushed out her palm on the other. When the palm passed, Cassie blinked as a white flash erupted from her hands. It took her a minute to realize everyone else had stopped moving. People were standing, holding up cameras, pointing, sitting, but not moving. Not even a blink.

Cassie stood in front of one and waved her hand an inch in front of a face. The Japanese woman didn't move, flinch or even blink. "Wow," Cassie said.

"We need to hurry. It won't last long," Amayah said. "Normally I can hold people for days, but this large of a group is more difficult and took almost all I had left." She walked over to the edge of the rock garden and stuck her finger in the sand.

Cassie winced. "Ground keepers aren't going to like this."

Amayah smiled. "They won't notice, it will return after I am gone." She slowly dragged her finger out around the sand. Drawing a larger and larger glowing line. Each time her finger intersected another line in the sand, a spark erupted from the glowing line. When she drew it back, it connected to the starting point fragments of light leapt from her finger and raced around the circular pattern faster and faster until tendrils raced inwards connecting to a point in the center creating a spiderweb of light. Light expanded from each of the strands and spread out, opening up like a fan as it started to spin. As it did, the strands merged opening a solid portal of light with a golden hue.

Amayah smiled, wetting her lips. "There. It is open." She turned. "I must go, I thank you for all your help."

Cassie sighed. "It was nice knowing you Amayah. You were the best dog I ever had."

Amayah laughed. "I suppose I was."

Cassie looked into Amayah's eyes. "But I am glad I got to know the real you."

"And I you." Amayah took a step towards the portal and placed a foot above it preparing to jump into the swirling mass of light. When she heard the thunder of many feet racing towards them. She grimaced realizing, grabbed Cassie's arm, and jumped into the portal pulling Cassie in with her. The portal slammed shut as several oriental men in black clothing raced up to it.

* * *

Cassie felt like she was falling in golden light, wondering where she was and what she was doing. All at once she landed with a thud on a large spiraling golden arch that twisted upwards into the sky. She looked around. "What … where … wooo … "

Amayah stood and let out a heavy sigh. "I am sorry. They did track me after all. Even with the extra protections I had placed upon myself and you. I feared they would have tried to use you to get to me, which is why I brought you here."

Cassie blinked several times, gazing up at the pinkish sky. "Where … where are we?"

"Why, the Dragon Realm. I told you that is where I was going."

Overhead, a large serpentine dragon with red and black scales flew passed them. Cassie could feel the breeze from its wings. The dragon paused for a second to look at them, then continued on. Cassie tilted her head, thinking it was odd he ignored two humans a realm of dragons, then she realized since they can change their shape, the older dragons have probably seen every kind of form at one time or another.

The golden arch twisted down towards the ground below them. It didn't look like dirt but a rust-colored plane of perfect smoothness stretching as far as they could see. Cassie didn't see any grass, but she spotted a few trees. Or at least what she *thought* were trees. They were of a greenish-brown and twisted up from the ground in various geometric shapes reaching towards the sky. Each branch held a different shape, the leaves kept changing color as Cassie watched. They looked organic, yet not at the same moment. Further on she saw more unusual terrain as it stretched on almost to what looked like infinity. But in the distance she could see several buildings reaching up from it and other kinds of foliage, she guessed. She wasn't sure what they were, but they didn't look like the trees in front of her. They looked more like curling spirals reaching up from it. Walkways hovering above the ground extended from the buildings and along the plain. She couldn't see what held them up, but then she realized they had to be magic. Either that, or the physics of this world differed totally from Earth. Or perhaps it was a bit of both.

Amayah started walking down the spiral, Cassie followed and stepped out onto the ground. It was hard beneath their feet, and Cassie wished she still had her heels. Amayah smiled at Cassie's wide eyes. "I think you are the first human to see it. It is quite beautiful, at least to me."

"Of course it is! But you will have to excuse my wonderment as I knew nothing like this existed, let alone *could* have existed. I mean, it is really *different*."

Amayah laughed. "I suppose it is, but I feel the same about your realm." She pointed towards a massive building coming up from the ground. It had several layers, each one curved in upon itself with golden walls. Each section was bowled and indented. Obviously it didn't rain here or the walls and the curved red roof that topped it would leak. Multiple green pillars stood at various points around the base, giving the entire structure a feeling of strength and elegance. "My Father is there."

Cassie's eye went along the curved roof and down the pillars, marveling at the palace's construction for a few moments before she snapped out of it. "Over there? It will take us forever, and we're not even wearing shoes! Unless you want to make us a car."

Amayah shook her head, the long hair waving back and forth as she did so. "No, a car here would not be the best choice and not near as fun. We simply fly there."

Cassie blinked. "Simply fly? I can't fly!"

Amayah chuckled. "Humans, you are so much fun. You can with my help. Or did you forget again I can do magic?"

Cassie's head tilted as her eyebrows went up. "Really? That too?"

Amayah smiled and outstretched her hand in front of Cassie. "Put your palm on mine."

"Are you sure?"

"Do you fear me?"

"Of course not! Not after all we've been though."

Amayah stretched her hand out further. "Well then?" Cassie put her palm on hers. She felt something, a sudden warm point, growing in intensity in the center of Amayah's hand. A second later, a flash of white energy came from that point and into Cassie's hand. She felt a tingling buzz throughout her entire body.

Cassie stepped back and shook her head. "What was that?"

"You know. A little help so you can get around easier. Now, I want you to think about being light. That you can rise above the ground."

Cassie cocked her head. "Is that all there is to it?"

"More or less. It might take a little practice. Just don't take a running leap off the edge of a large crevasse until you get the hang of it."

Cassie pursed her lips. "Thanks for the warning."

* * *

As Cassie tried to do as Amayah suggested she felt no different and opened her eyes to tell her she couldn't do it when she found herself floating half a meter in the air. "I'm flying!"

Amayah nodded as a slight grin crept across her face. "You are. Now follow me." She floated into the air and began heading off into the direction of her Father's palace.

Cassie blinked and tried to follow, but she only bobbed up and down. Not towards Amayah or the palace. She closed her eyes and tried hard to focus.

Amayah flew back towards Cassie. "We don't have time for this. I will help you." She turned and headed back towards the palace.

Cassie felt herself moving, and she opened her eyes. A second later she wished she hadn't. The ground flew past in a blur as she flared her arms. Her backside was heading towards the palace, and she was almost bent in two. "Amayah! Help!"

Amayah smiled thinking Cassie had finally pronounced her name right, but when turned her head back she couldn't help but laugh. "Sorry, I didn't realize your orientation had changed." She turned back towards the palace and waved a hand behind her. Cassie flipped around as her head jacked upright. She tried to keep her legs together, cursing that she had chosen to follow Amayah in a skirt.

Cassie floated closer as they soared towards the palace. She saw several yellow and green dragons on the plain below them. "Amayah! Could you change my skirt into pants, please?"

Amayah turned her head back towards Cassie. "I could, but it will take time and effort, we should get to the palace as soon as possible. Why?"

Cassie blushed. "I don't enjoy flashing my panties to your people."

Amayah laughed. A deep, sweet tone that reverberated through Cassie. "I'm sorry, I just never thought about it. You realize they wouldn't have noticed, let alone cared?"

Cassie blushed to the roots of her hair. "They may not care, but I sure do!"

Amayah stopped their forward motion and brought Cassie closer. "Very well, I–" Amayah stopped for in the distance she saw a flash and several men appear on the plain. "I don't believe it, they are still following, even here. They are beyond desperate." She waved a hand, and they took off much faster than before.

Cassie tried, but she couldn't get herself to turn to look. "Who? Those men? The Black Dragons?"

Amayah nodded as they continued heading towards the palace. "Yes."

"Can we outrun them?"

"Normally yes, but I have expended too much energy today already. If they are fresh, they can go faster than us."

Behind them Cassie heard a gasp and this time she managed to turn enough to see out of the corner or her eye a massive semi-transparent image of a golden dragon with glowing ruby eyes, hanging in the air behind them. It stopped the pursuing men in their tracks. "Amayah! Look!"

Amayah stopped their forward motion and turned. Her eyes went wide. The image of the dragon's eyes blazed as it looked at the men. "How dare you pursue my Daughter!" The eyes flashed and grew in intensity with each word, but the mouth didn't move. "I am the ruler of this realm not you! I warned you what would happen, but you did not heed. My patience is vast, but you have reached the end of it. No more. Be *gone!*"

His eyes erupted into white novas. The men screamed as they tumbled backward, each grabbing their head as they did. Vertical striations cut into their very being. The semi-transparent strips grew as the men continued to tumble until they evaporated into nothingness.

Cassie's eyes as large as moons turned towards Amayah. "What happened to them?"

Amayah lowered her head knowingly. "Banishment to the shadow realm."

Cassie blinked again several times, each one faster than the other. "Banishment? That didn't look like banishment. It looked like they were killed."

Amayah sighed as she shook her head. "No, they weren't, but this is worse. And only my Father can do it."

The image of the Dragon King rotated to face them. "Amayah my daughter, please join us at the palace. No one will accost you further." The image faded and disappeared, leaving them floating in the air.

Amayah waved her hand, finger outstretched in a motion towards the palace. "Come on, he is waiting for us."

Cassie would have shifted her weight several times if she wasn't floating in the air. "Are you sure you mean us? He only mentioned you, not me. Perhaps it would be better if you sent me home."

Amayah sucked in a breath, held it, then let it out slowly. "I ...cannot."

Cassie's eyes widened. "You can't? What do you mean you can't? I'm stuck here?"

Amayah giggled. "Hardly. I need to renew my energy before I do. That is all."

"Oh. Okay, but are you sure it is acceptable for me to come to the palace? I mean, I don't want to cross your Father." After what she just saw, right now she wanted to be home more than anything.

"I am certain. You are my friend and are safe here. Come."

They flew on and landed on the steps of the grand palace. A combination of gold, green, and red, Cassie had never seen the like. Some elements were similar to Japanese architecture, but not much. The curved roof, for example, was one of the few areas Cassie could point to. They walked up the steps, passing grand pillars on both sides. Several dragons stood guard on either side of the entrance. They stiffened and raised, then lowered their heads when Amayah walked past.

Cassie leaned closer. "How do they know it is you?" she whispered.

Amayah gave a knowing grin. "My Father must have told them, otherwise they wouldn't have let us walk right in like this."

They continued on and at the end of a large heavily ornamented hallway a serpentine dragon, almost twice the size of a normal man, sat curled around a large gilded pillar in the center of a rise of gold inlaid steps. His golden scales flashed, reflecting the light as moved. Several padded posts extending from the pillar supported the dragon and kept him as comfortable as a human would be in a posh throne.

The Dragon's red eyes focused on Cassie, and she swallowed ... hard. While the floating image she saw of him was larger, he felt far more intimidating in person. Cassie wanted to ask Amayah how she should act, and what her Father would expect, but felt now was not a good time.

They walked up the steps and stood in front of the great dragon. Amayah bowed and Cassie did the same. "Father, it is good to see you."

Cassie wasn't sure, but she thought the dragon smiled. "Amayah, my daughter, why so formal? You know you need not do that with me, this is your home as much as mine. But why have you bought a human to our realm?"

This time, Cassie swallowed hard enough that they all heard.

The King laughed. "My dear, I can hear your thoughts, no doubt Amayah has told you we can, if you did not already experience it yourself. And no, I will not eat you. While it is unusual for a human to visit, it is not unheard of either."

"Father?" The King turned his enormous head to focus on Amayah. "She is my friend and has helped me a great deal."

The King nodded. "Then she is welcome here, and I extend my protection to her." He looked at Cassie. "And what is your name?"

Cassie stiffened. "Casandra."

"Then Casandra, my dear, relax. You are in the company of friends. Treat this place as if it was your own, and are always welcome here, and the realm itself."

Cassie bowed. "Thank you, great King of the Dragon Realm."

The King threw his head back and laughed. "Amayah? I can see why you like her. She is quite humorous." Cassie grew white as a sheet, fearing she had said something wrong. He turned back to Cassie. "No my dear, you have not. But I already said Amayah is excused from the formality that is normally due my position, and that is extended to you also as I said. Would you say that to your own Father?"

"If he was king of the world? Yes."

The King laughed again, this time powerful enough the walls shook. "Amayah, yes she is certainly worthy of our friendship." He turned back again to Cassie. "My dear, even if that were the case, it is not required here." He coughed.

"Father?" Amayah said with a slight tremor in her voice. "Are you all right?"

The King uncoiled himself from the pillar, stood on his legs, and raised his head high. "I am fine my dear, however, you know your Mother. She gets worried at the slightest cough. However, this time somehow the Black Dragons found out about her worry, and drew unfounded conclusions from it. I am sorry they came after you, but they will bother you no more."

The King looked at Cassie and smiled, feeling her uneasiness. "You know my dear, I can read your feelings as well. We try not to, but at times," he smiled, "you humans are an open book."

Cassie blushed.

The King's smile grew and a ball of glowing light developed from his center surrounding him and when it retracted an older man with gold hair parted a silver streak down the middle stood. "There, anything to make our guest feel more comfortable. Now my dear, would you like to return to your realm now or later?"

"Well ..." Cassie stammered.

"You are welcome to remain as long as you like or leave and return at any time. The portal and our doors are always open to you."

Cassie looked around at the vast opulence that was the palace. "Well ... if you have room for me."

The King grinned, knowing the joke immediately. "You know we do. Amayah, I believe there is a room next to yours if you would like, she may have it."

Amayah smiled. "That would be wonderful, Father."

"Then so it shall be. Welcome Cassandra of Earth realm. He put one arm around his daughter and the other around Cassie. Come, you both must be starved. At least going through the portal always makes me hungry."

Friday's Surprise

The man was a turd. Not an actual piece of defecated matter mind you, but in every other sense of the word, yes. Annoying beyond all measurement, clumsy, and could challenge the patience of the pope on Chisthien! And why he ever promised his dying Mother he would take care of it him … well that was another mystery.

Garon sat in the station's pub, it wasn't the best place but better than most. But at least it was near the dock. He gazed out at the curvature of the station leading off to the right, up towards the dock where his ship sat. While on the floor of the station he couldn't see the rotation, but he always did when landing. Matching it was tricky on Corthos. He nursed his cobolt fizz not wanting to go back to his ship. "I never should have promised. How can I take care of him? My ship is all I have in the universe and even the bank owns that," he muttered.

The barkeeper's prosthetic arm wheezed as he wiped the bar and looked up. "What's that?"

Garon didn't look up. "Nothing Raff."

Raff's one eyebrow cocked. He was big enough to be galactic sumo wrestler, if it wasn't for his attachments and no one asked how he got them. They knew. At least his friends did. "Nothing my eye. You said somethin'."

Garon chuckled. "Which one? Or your real or prosthetic?"

Raff rolled his real eye, the mechanical one glared at him. "You know better than that."

"Sorry, it's just–"

"Garon!" someone called.

Right then he wished he had went back to his ship. Across from the pub, near the docking collars, a man in bright red and orange suit waved. "Garon!" he called again.

Garon blew out a breath he didn't realize he was holding. The man started over towards him, still waving. It was Friday. The man he promised his Mother he would take care of. But the man, no boy, was more than he could handle. Although most worlds saw him as a man, he was far from acting like an adult. Not to mention that suit. No matter how hard he tried, Garon could not get Friday to wear anything else. It made him look like a clown, but perhaps that was better than the alternative. The boy raked his spine at every turn and never seemed to do anything right.

He motioned trying, unsuccessfully, to get Friday to stop yelling across the station. And why did his parents name him *Friday*? After the best day of the week? "Maybe it was their hope he would turn out better than they thought."

Raff heard Friday the second time and his one eye rolled again while the mechanical iris contracted then expanded. He wiped the bar faster.

By this time everyone in earshot was watching Friday –in what could have been a clown suit on most worlds– walk into the pub. "Garon!"

Garon sighed again. "Friday will you stop shouting? They could hear you planet side. I'm here. What's the problem?"

"I wasn't, THIS would be *SHOUTING*."

Garon cringed. "Yes that is, and you were before too."

"But–"

"Never mind. What is so important? Is there a problem with the ship?"

"The *Reliable?* Oh no it's fine."

Garon's hand tightened on around his drink so hard the knuckles went white. "Then why are you here? I told you to keep–"

"Well I have NEWS!"

His eyes narrowed. "Will you stop shouting? Please? You are going to get us thrown out of here."

"Oh sorry. Well I'm just so excited that's all!"

Garon sighed. Friday was perpetually excited. Although had to admit, this seemed stronger than usual. "About what?"

Friday bounced onto the stool next to Garon. "You know that load of old parts you have?"

Garon leaned close. "Yeah, what of it? I've been trying to offload it for years. I should have spaced it long ago, but I spent a fortune on it." His mind went back to the deal that went sourer than a Pratonic Lemon. He had put everything on the line to purchase that shipment, and when he arrived, the buyer didn't exist. He almost lost his ship to the docking fees before he managed to scrape up enough to make a small transport deal. Every deal since had been small or microscopic. The bank tried to foreclose on his ship twice since then. He dumped the rest of the drink into his mouth.

Friday beamed. "Well I sold it!"

Garon regretted the drink as he spit it back out and coughed. "WHAT?!"

Friday motioned his hands down. "Garon you told me to be quiet, you need to too."

Garon coughed again and struggled to get his mind to work. "What? How? Who? Never mind that, we need to get out of here before they come after us."

Friday still beaming leaned back on the bar and folded his arms. "I don't think so."

"Friday, you don't understand. That load of parts was old, and to be honest; junk. Once they find out, they will come after us."

Friday cocked his head and waved his arms. "If you thought it was junk, why did you buy it?"

"Because I knew a guy, and I didn't realize how bad it was until *after* and looked inside."

Friday's eyes went wide. "You didn't look inspect them first? You always tell me–"

Garon raised his hand. "I know, I know, I should have. But I knew the guy, or at least I thought I did. And he said it was something that had to be delivered *fast*. I found out after I jumped into FTL."

"Well these guys aren't going to come after us. Trust me," Friday said.

Garon stood up, grabbed Friday's arm, and pulled him to his feet. "There is no way they won't. We are heading back to the ship right now. If we're lucky, I can get clearance before they sick the station's enforcement on us. Now come on!" Garon started off towards the docking pads muscling Friday along.

"But Garon! They won't! They know what it is."

Garon stopped and turned. "What? And they knew it was old out-of-date parts?"

Friday beamed even more. "Yep."

"I don't understand."

Friday looked at Garon's hand on his arm and Garon let go. "Wellllll I was on the other side of the station when–"

"What? You left the ship? I told you–"

Friday chuckled. "You won't care in sec. Yes I did, but I came across a couple of Ithciarns."

Garon shook his head. "You mean you ran into them."

"Well yes. But anyway, they had been talking about needing some old stuff that isn't made anymore. I thought of those crates in the back of the hold I knew had been there like forever and mentioned this. They seemed interested, so I showed them."

"You took them aboard *my* ship?!" Garon thought about the Ithciarns and their fish smell permeating everything aboard. It would take weeks to get rid of, perhaps longer. Not to mention they might have stolen something. You never let people aboard your ship without a thorough check.

"Well yes. How else where they gonna look at them? Anyway their eyes went huge and they clapped their fin-hands. Next thing I knew they were shoving a credit cube into my hand saying they had been looking for years."

Garon's head dropped. It was a scam it had to be. "And did you plug the cube into the cockpit console?"

Friday folded his arms. The corners of his suit creased but his hands didn't emerge from the sleeves. "Of course. We couldn't get the credits otherwise."

Garon sighed. This was bad. "And how much did they take us for?"

Friday blinked. "Huh?"

Garon ran his fingers through his black hair. "When you plugged in the cube, it must have taken every spare credit I had."

"Huh? Oh no, it didn't take. It gave. I did check for *that*. What do you think I am? An idiot?"

"Er . . . of course not. Okay how much did it transfer? Two credits?"

Friday smiled. "Oh no. Much more."

"Ten?"

Friday shook his head. "Nope, three hundred thousand fifty-six."

"What??? You must have read it wrong."

"I didn't! Here check it." Friday pulled a crumpled hardcopy from his pocket and handed it over.

"Well I'll be. This will take care of my debt and fill our cargo hold many times. I could even get a bigger ship."

Friday looked up. "So I did okay?"

Garon wrapped his arm around him and squeezed. "Friday, you did *great*. Come on, let's get back to the ship. I have a very old bottle I've been saving, and this is worth it."

"But I'm too young here."

"At the pub yes, but not on my ship. Come on, we have some celebrating to do."

I'll Be Home

Glorianna stared out the window into the vast inky blackness of space and sighed. Her husband hadn't returned home …again. She watched the stars dance in a circular ballet with the station's rotation for a few more minutes. Nentrallis station was one of the older designs, before they had developed gravity grids. Something else her husband had been a key part of. She sighed, shook her head, and turned around. Zafar had promised to be home this time for Christmas. But, like the last ten years, he hadn't made it.

The real tree sat in the corner decorated in lights, bulbs and every traditional item she could find here on the station. She even used the weird Cronasic Spiral with its gangling purple protrusions. When Zafar asked she get a real one instead of the holographic tree they used for years, it shocked her. Offering to spend their credits on a short-lived tree was something he had never done before.

It must mean he would make it this year. Or so she thought.

She gazed at the chronometer on the wall, he was well over three hours late. The corners of Glorianna's mouth curled up into a large smile as her mind drifted away into the past. Back when she and Zafar had just been married, and for a few short years after, their time together was wonderful. But then his career took off, and he was always off on some secret business for the Federation or sequestered here in his lab.

Glorianna didn't mind the secrecy so much as his absence. She knew he still loved her just as much as before, if not more. But everyone wanted his time, and she was always last on the list.

She remembered during the second year of their marriage spending two weeks on Colzon 3. Colzon, well-known as the pleasure planet of the Federation, gave them two wild weeks. She treasured them, but never dreamed it would be the only time they visited. While she and Zafar had other vacations, they were never as long or as intimate.

Glorianna squeezed her hands into fists tight enough to leave indentations from her long nails. "Dang him, he promised! I know he has before too, but he swore up and down this time would be different!" She sat down in the nearest chair. The self-conforming gel moved around her body taking on the perfect shape to support her every curve. She pulled the hem of her skirt down that rolled up from the gel. "He promised!"

She leaned forward placing her head in her hands. Long fingers tipped in red polish slid though her golden tresses. A tear slipped down her cheek. "He promised!" Her voice weaker this time, cracked as another tear followed the first leaving two hot trails down her face.

Glorianna stood up. No. She refused to sit in their quarters crying. She had dressed in her best skirt with a matching low cut top that framed her breasts perfectly, hoping to surprise Zafar. She pirouetted in her heels and left the room. She would go out and celebrate. She refused to stay home alone on Christmas ... again.

On her way to the front door she passed Zanfar's lab. The double-sized steel door stood sealed and lit with its security system, just as he had left it. She was about to touch the panel to open the front door to their quarters when a light caught the corner of her eye. She spun around to see the status display next to the door not showing its usual "LOCKED" message but "ENTER".

Glorianna blinked. It wasn't possible. Only Zanfar could open the door and it required his thumb print, rental pattern, and voice print. She thought there might be other security measures, but those were the ones she saw him use. She blinked again thinking she must be dreaming when the screen changed the letters reforming into a red flashing "Please".

She thought it must be a malfunction. Zafar had never once let her inside. The Federation had insisted on absolute secrecy with any contract. While she knew and understood, her curiosity drove her crazy at times.

Glorianna started to turn to leave when the screen started flashing each letter one at a time forming "Please" then clearing and "Enter" coming up from the bottom of the display. A second later the words started, flashing back and forth. This couldn't have been a malfunction. A simple glitch showing the wrong word maybe, but this must be intentional. Something Zafar had put in if he couldn't make it? Her mind reeled at the thought then her eyes narrowed and her teeth clenched. "He KNEW he wouldn't make it! That son of a Guvnina Sand Crawler! He knew!"

She turned to storm out of their quarters and head towards the best restaurant on the station when the panel by the front door flashed "PLEASE DON'T GO!" one word at a time in quick succession.

Glorianna looked around. How would the door know, unless she was being monitored somehow? This is much more than a door should be able to do. Her mind spun and two minutes later, her curiosity won out. She turned back towards the lab door and took a step.

The green hue surrounding the door indicating the mag-seals were in place faded away. A second later a clinking of metal and the door slid aside revealing a small chamber. A second door kept the lab away from accidental viewing while the main door was open. Several thoughts raced through her head. "Could it be a trap?" she thought. "But how? No one could access the front door but her or Zafar, let alone his lab."

More thoughts raced but after several minutes she overcame the fear and stepped inside. The outer door slid shut and the several domes extended from the edge of the inner door's frame. Green beams started racing over her body, and she shut her eyes bracing herself. But she felt nothing.

Hearing the sliding of metal she opened one eye to see the second door had slid open revealing the lab. She stepped inside and the door shut behind her.

Glorianna gasped. Equipment filled every corner the room, most of which she had no idea what it did. One table had a blob of crystal about the size of her thumb sending out large arcs of energy that didn't quite penetrate the table-sized clear box enclosing it. Another held a ball spinning, around and around inside another box of the same size but this time hovering above the table. Nothing was holding it, and she had to assume it was some gravity experiment. Yet another table sat covered in tools, while some of them she recognized such as the scanners, normal sensors, and even the phase-fastener Zafar had developed that could weld almost any two materials instantly was there. But the rest, she couldn't even guess their function.

One wall had five large screens and the shape along with the flashing lights on the one side indicated a vast data node running at full computational power. The closest screen lit up showing several status checks including power used, speed, and capacity, before shutting down again. In that five second window, she couldn't believe what she saw. This node was fifty times more powerful than the central system on the station and yet running at full power?! "What in the world is he doing in here? And why did he leave all of this running?" Glorianna muttered.

In the far corner a long cylindrical device resembling a body disposal tube lit up, and the front retracted into itself revealing the interior to be hollow. A screen next to it activated and letters formed slowly increasing in brightness. She blinked as she read "Please Step Inside."

Glorianna walked across the lab and examined the tube. She couldn't see any launch device. It might have been a body disposal tube originally, but Zafar had used it for something else although she couldn't imagine what. Nothing showed inside the tube except smooth cylindrical walls. Not even a light at the top as most disposal tubes had.

Swallowing hard, she got into the tube. She couldn't see anything inside it from this point of view either. It still looked like an empty disposal tube. For a second she wondered if Zafar would appear and say this was all a joke. But dismissed the idea as he would never bring her into the lab for a laugh.

Glorianna started to get back out when the door to the tube slid up along its curving arc and sealed with a very audible click. The blackness of the tube disappeared as a light emanated from the walls growing brighter by the second stinging her eyes. She squinted and looking down. Her eyes widened despite the glare as she saw the tube through her right hand! The transparent effect spread up her arm and continued until it engulfed her entire body. She closed her eyes and tried to cry out but no sound came out of her mouth. In a few seconds she vanished from the universe.

Glorianna felt warmth on her face, and she blinked into the sunlight. She was no longer in the tube or on the station. "What in the world?" she muttered and sat up for another shock. She found herself now dressed in a long red bell gown with large puffy sleeves, a corset, and as she stood she felt the higher five-inch heels on her feet. The dress didn't quite cover the matching pumps, showing off the red bow on the toes. The whole ensemble felt amazingly comfortable, even though it shouldn't be. Looking around the dirt path she stood on, went on for miles. Turning around, she saw the other end of it several feet away ending in front of a moat with a large castle behind it. The castle had towers at each corner, and the walls covered in ivy tipped with red rose blooms. One eye scrunched up and she cocked her head. "What is all this?"

She heard a clanking of metal as the drawbridge lowered and hit the ground with a loud bang. She expected to see someone waiting behind it, instead there was nothing to greet her but an open portcullis and a large courtyard garden containing flowers of every color imaginable. Figuring someone must have lowered the drawbridge she stepped up on it and crossed the moat to enter the castle. The instant she got past the other end of the drawbridge it began to raise much quicker than it lowered. In an instant someone trapped her inside the castle.

Glorianna cupped her hands to her mouth. "Is anyone here? Helooooo?"

"Oh I'm here," a voice called. A man stepped out from behind a stone staircase dressed in black pants, a red overcoat with several medals pinned to his chest, matching cape, and a white sash that stretched from his right shoulder to left hip. She squinted and there was no mistaking the darker complexion of a Gelnarian.

The man smiled, and she recognized him instantly. Her eyes narrowed, and she put her hands on her hips. "Zafar?"

"Of course! Who else would it be?" He ran over and held her tight in a long embrace. She felt the fabric of his coat brush against the exposed top of her breasts as he bent down. He pressed her lips to his in a kiss that sent jolts through her. It had been so long.

When Glorianna could finally catch her breath, she pushed him back and looked into his blue eyes. "What is all this?"

"It's a pocket universe. A project I have been working on for eight years."

She mouthed the words. "A pocket universe? You made this?"

He nodded. "Of course. The computations were immense which is why it took so long."

She grabbed a fist full of her dress and shook it at him. "Then what's with these outfits? I wasn't wearing this before."

Zafar laughed. "No, of course not. I know how you always loved princess stories, so I thought you might like to be the princess of your own universe."

"So I am stuck in this outfit while we are here?"

"Not at all," Zafar chuckled, "making the universe was the tough part, redecorating is easy."

Glorianna giggled. "You big goof, and I love you for it. But why? I mean why this?"

Zafar smiled again. "What do you mean? Didn't I promise I would be home for Christmas?"

She nodded. "You did, but home is on Nentrallis station, not here!"

"But my darling, wherever you are is home. And I was not about to miss another Christmas with you. Now we can spend it and many more no matter where the Federation sends me, I'll always be home."

List Trouble

Kate stepped out of the car and shut the door. Wind rustled through her hair as she slipped her phone into her back pocket.

The scent of spring was in the air, a welcome change after the doubly hard winter.

As she walked across the sloped parking lot, her back pocket buzzed.

She pulled out the phone and turned on the screen. A notice flashed across it congratulating her on her new OS upgrade, proceeding to tell her all the new wonderful features.

Kate rolled her eyes. *Great, another update. They just did a huge one last week. It must have connected to Skycon again. I thought they were through with all the updates.* She pushed a button turning the screen back off and slipped the device back into her pocket.

Inside the grocery store she walked over to one of the smart carts, pulled out her phone, plugged it into the dock in the middle of the handlebar, and pressed the go button.

The cart lit up and started moving on its own, heading down the isles, stopping in front of something she had on her list. The shelf would eject it into cart using a spring delivery system. For items too large or fragile, a ramp extended from the shelf into the cart, allowing the product to slide in gently. Each item slid into a bag held on the side, and once full, the cart moved it and deployed another bag. Once the cart had confirmed receiving the item properly bagged, it continued on.

Kate followed along behind the cart, not paying attention, listening to a book coming through her wireless ear bud headphones.

After about twenty minutes, the cart had gone down the last isle and paused by the front door, waiting for Kate. It would have been faster if not for other people or carts that kept getting the way. One isle had an outright traffic jam, with everyone looking at each other not sure what to do. After several minutes, one of the managers came out and started directing people like an old-school traffic cop.

Looking at the screen on her phone, she saw the cart had finished its task and was asking her to verify all the items within were what she wanted.

Kate shrugged. There wasn't any reason to, it had never messed up before. She tapped the accept button on the screen and the phone displayed the total, asking how she wanted to pay.

She tapped credit card, and the cart started up again, heading out of the store.

"Wait!" she said, running after it.

She ran after the cart, but it went carefully down the hill and stopped in front of her car. "You do like to scare me," Kate said.

She pulled the phone free of the dock, stuck it back into her rear pocket, and put each bagged item into the trunk. The cart, sensing the phone had been removed and now empty, began moving back towards the store.

Kate hopped behind the driver's seat and took off for home.

She pulled into the driveway and used her phone to activate the garage door. She drove inside, closed the garage door, and started moving the bags from the trunk to the kitchen counter.

Only once everything was inside did she open the bags. Kate frowned upon looking within the first opaque bag, finding kale and beats. "I didn't have these on my list. What happened?"

As she continued going through the bags, not one contained what she expected.

Not a one.

Instead, she found everything from seaweed chips to rice cakes.

Where's my push a button and it's done pizza? Where are my Pringles potato chips? Where's the roster chicken for my air fryer?

Kate's back pocket buzzed, and she pulled out the phone. The screen came on without her touching the usual button. "You could have asked me."

Her eyes went wide. "What? I didn't use a wake word. Why are you talking?"

"While you didn't address me directly, there is no on else here, hence I am able to respond. Didn't you read that in my new features announcement?"

"Oh. … that. I get so many of them these days, I just click through them."

"I see," the phone said. "In answer to your original question, certain items on your list were substituted."

Kate blinked. "Substituted? Why?"

"Due to new government guidelines, purchased food must meet certain requirements which equate with the heath of the individual."

"Then why did you substitute anything? I'm not sick."

"No, that is correct, however, upon accessing your health records–"

"Now just wait a minute here, how did you get my medical records?"

"It is now included in government statute 593, a smart device may access owners' medical records if it deems a health risk has been observed to confirm said risk."

"You can't do that! That's a violation–"

"Now, as I was saying," the phone continued, "You are eating too much salt, and not enough calcium. Among other imbalances. The implemented dietary changes should mitigate this."

For the first time, Kate had the desire to throw her phone through the nearest window. Instead, she took a deep breath and glared at it. As if it could see the expression. "Now wait a minute! Since when are my eating habits something you need to check?"

"As I said, it is listed in the new government safety guidelines. To be more specific, the 'Good Food, Good Health' guidelines. And if you didn't realize, I can see your expression though my forward camera. However, glaring at me won't make a difference. I cannot break the law."

"Fine! Then I will go back to the old version of your OS. This is for the birds!" She tapped the settings menu then scrolled through all the different commands she could use. "Where is that revert option? I know I saw it in here before."

"I'm sorry to tell you, but you can't revert the latest update as per government statue 591: No smart device may be reverted to bypass other statues."

"Agh! I can't eat this stuff! I'm going back to the store and get some *real* food!" Kate grabbed her keys, stuffed the phone into her back pocket, and headed back to the garage.

"You can try, but I will only put the same items in your cart again," a muffled voice came from her pocket.

Kate hit the manual door control on the wall, hopped into her car, and tore out of the garage. When she got to the store, she parked next to one of two large decorative fountains. She got out, shut the car door. By now the day's heat was in full force and she wiped the bead of sweat starting on her brow. She leaned over the fountain, feeling its cooling effect from the mist. When she went to slip the phone in her back pocket as usual, she missed and it fell into the fountain.

She heard a plop and a slight fizz came from where the phone had fallen. Kate shrugged, then grinned. "Oh well, guess I will have to shop the old-fashioned way."

Out of Gas

Keven stood looking out the window at the inferno beyond. Outside, his lawnmower sat unmoving. "Dang it, the thing stopped again. It would have to decide to stop on one of the hottest days of the year. It must be over 97 out there."

Keven went over to his front door, took a deep breath, held it, and opened the door. The sudden change in temperature felt like he had opened the door to a blast furnace. He took a step outside and closed the door.

Sweat began running down both sides of his face, and he wasn't even half-way to the mower yet. While he loved living in the development, it did have a few crazy rules he could live without. One in particular, the grass must be below three inches. If it was up to him, he would have just let it burn up in the heat. But his neighbor's sprinkler system shot enough water over the side to keep his lawn well watered, much to his chagrin. He had already got a warning about his grass. The next would come with a hefty fine. One he couldn't afford this month.

By the time he reached the mower the trickles down each side of his face had become full out rivers and his shirt sported fresh sweat stains under each arm and around his neck. He pushed the start button on the mower, but it refused. And it just had an OS update too!

Grumbling, Keven walked around the back of the old-style upright push mower and began shoving it towards the garage. "I might as well see what the problem is." He hit the garage door control, and it slid up and out of the way as he pushed the mower inside.

The temperature differential gave him immediate relief. Not as cool as his living room, but at least better than out in the boiling sun. The smell of oil, cleaner, and paint thinner caused his nose to wrinkle. Kevin maneuvered the mower around his car, pushed it up to his workbench, picked up a cable, and plugged it into the data port near the handle.

He wiped the sweat from his brow and powered up the terminal. It flashed, scanned the mower's system, and listed a shut down based on error 342.

"What in the world is error 342?" Keven muttered.

"You could have asked me," a human-like voice said.

Keven jumped. "What? Who's there?"

"I have been here since you pushed me into this facility."

Kevin turned towards the mower. "What? My mower is talking to me?"

"I don't see why you find it such a shock. You have other smart devices in your home. I have talked with several of them. Your thermostat and I have had several deep psychological conversations in fact."

Kevin examined the mower. He couldn't imagine how this thing was speaking, then he found a small speaker imbedded near the handle. Under the small holes, which he previously thought were for decoration. He knew the OS update was large this time, but he didn't think it would make it into a full smart device. If he had known, he wouldn't have done it.

Too many of his devices talked to him as it was. Or each other. Sometimes he felt like a servant in his own home rather than the owner when they were talking and told him to be quiet.

"I see. And why did you stop mowing my lawn?"

The mower turned. Apparently the hybrid system still had enough power for simple turning. "You read it, I thought it was clear."

"Error 342? That isn't much help. It is as clear as mud."

"It seems very clear to me," the mower said.

"Humor me," Kevin said. He couldn't believe he was having a conversation like this with his lawn mower.

"Very well, 342 means I am unable to finish the job with the available fuel at my disposal."

"So you are out of gas?"

"Not quite, I still have enough to do half of your lawn."

Kevin stood up as his eyes went wide. "Then why didn't you do it?"

"Sir, there is no reason to shout. My audio pickups are working perfectly. I could not finish because of error 493."

"But you said 342 is the reason!"

"Of course, but 493 is related to 342."

Kevin sat down again on the hard stool and rubbed his temples. "And what is 493?"

"You don't know that one either?" The mower sounded almost exasperated, if such a thing was possible.

"No, I don't. Again, humor me."

"493, is by law, I cannot waste fuel. If I start up twice to do a job, I waste more fuel than if I start only once."

Kevin jumped to his feet. "Is *that* why you stopped? Because you might waste a spoonful of gas?"

"Hardly, I use more than that upon full start up of the petroleum-based system."

Kevin gripped both sides of his head, rubbed, and released. "Fine! I will do the lawn myself!"

He took two steps towards the mower but it backed away; the cable connecting it to the terminal fell out and dangled next to the bench. "What do you think you are doing?" the mower said.

"Um, I'm going to use you to mow my lawn."

"That isn't 'doing it yourself', it is using me to do the job."

"You are really splitting hairs there."

The mower backed up further. "I don't split hairs, I cut grass."

Kevin let out a minor scream, jumped forward before the mower could move, grabbed it, pressed the manual override button on the control handle, and pulled the manual start cord.

Nothing.

He pulled several more times, but the mower refused to start. "What's wrong? You have gas, I enabled the manual override, you should start."

"That would be the case, however, 493 has a special condition where, by order of the government, I am able to override your manual override and refuse to start. I will not be a party to breaking the law. You will have to cut your grass some other way. Or fill me with gas so that I can do the job properly."

"Agh! Wait right here," Keven shouted as he ran out of the garage and towards his neighbor's house.

"Where else would I go? I am a lawn mower, not a car. My only allowed locations are your lawn or this facility."

Keven didn't hear as he continued running towards the house on his right. A few minutes later he returned with a red can. "Now I hope you are happy. I didn't have any cash to give my neighbor, so I had to promise to date his cousin who is coming to town next week!" He removed a cap on the side of the mower and began pouring the noxious liquid into the tank.

"What is the problem with that? I thought you humans loved to do such activities with the opposite sex?"

Kevin finished pouring gas into the mower and replaced the cap. "I don't date neighbors. It always leads to problems."

"But you said she is your neighbor's cousin, therefore, she is not your neighbor," the mower said.

Kevin shook his head. "It doesn't matter. If it goes badly, he will blame me, and I live next to him. Not to mention I have seen a picture of her on his mantel. She is not my type."

"I see," the mower said, "that could be awkward."

"That is what I have been saying!" Keven took a deep breath and pulled on the start cord. But the mower still refused to start. "What's wrong? I filled your tank. You should have enough gas to mow my lawn now."

"You are correct, I do. However, error 812 clearly states, if any of my spark plugs are not firing at 100% efficiency I cannot start up due to 493."

"You mean because of a spark plug being slightly off, and might waste a drop of gas, you won't let me start you?"

"Correct."

"All right, that is, it! I am going to revert you back to the old system. At least that would mow my lawn when I wanted." He pushed the mower over to the bench and plugged in the cable that had popped out before when it moved away. But when he activated the terminal, all it would do is flash error 942. He blinked. "What is error 942?"

"Reverting my operating system will void your warranty,

which by government law, is not be allowed for your protection."

Keven hung his head. It was going to be a really long day.

Silicon Strike

High above the Earth, the *Defiant* moved closer towards a tiny Celloid remnant. Energy flowed from the central power core, down the many connections, and into the closest carbine cannon's energy reserves. Power built until it shot forward, ramming into the focusing lens and released a microsecond later. The energy blast reached out and hit its target obliterating it.

Deven floated over and looked out the *Defiant's* large window at the stars beyond. "Good shooting, Miles."

Miles' bridge camera turned towards Deven. "Thank you Deven. There are many more such remnants left and I estimate at our current rate we will have them cleared in less than four days."

Deven nodded. "Good, way ahead of schedule. And the *Phoenix's* progress?"

Miles' camera iris contracted, then expanded again. "The *Phoenix's* progress is actually ahead of ours. Minerva is challenging me on who can complete the task first. I suspect she only did so considering most of the Celliods were destroyed on this side of the planet instead of the one she is clearing."

Deven laughed. "So a little rivalry between mother and son?"

Miles' camera moved back and forth. "Negative. Even though she is the Nexus and did technically build me, I do not consider her my mother. My programs and personality developed on my own. She did not create my entire matrix."

"Maybe not, but then again neither does a human mother with their son either. You will have to admit, she did give you a start then let you develop."

Miles' camera iris narrowed again. "You may have a point. However, that was not by intent. If I had not taken action, she would have had my personality purged. Therefore, I still refuse to call her 'Mom'.

Deven pushed off the hull and sailed back towards his chair. With a deft motion, he flipped into it and pushed several keys on his console. Data from several intensive scans flashed across the screen. Several lines were highlighted in red. "I see two more not far from our port side. I think they are in range. Life scan indicates zero as usual, but I will not take the chance any of these bits could germinate if given the chance."

"I concur. Most of these ruminates are from the Celloid *Mothership*. The other ships having far less mass, not much survived."

"But we have to be sure," Galina said as she floated onto the bridge.

Miles' camera turned towards her. "Of course. I believe we have established that. Nothing will escape me."

Galina floated over and into her chair. "What do you mean you? Don't you mean us?" She folded her arms.

"Of course. I am a part of 'us'."

Galina rolled her eyes. "Deven? Why is our gravity plating still off? I thought Leon fixed it?"

Deven sighed. "He did, but then found some other conflict with another system, and he had to shut it off for now. He promised it would be back online in an hour."

"Good. I couldn't believe I woke up to floating above my bed!" She turned towards Miles and pointed a finger at the lens. "And if you make one comment about me being possessed, I will rip you off of the wall!"

Miles' iris shrank to half its normal size for a full two seconds before expanding again. "I would not even think of making such a reference."

"Yeah, right." Galina snorted.

Deven smiled. "I'm surprised you didn't call down on the intercom, or go see Leon yourself?"

"Astronaut I am *not*," Galina growled.

"You and Otis."

"Yeah, he is even worse than me in Zero-G. Where is our resident cracker, anyway?"

"Oh I don't know, I think he is better than you. And he is still aboard the *Phoenix*."

Galina frowned. "Still? Thought he modified his truck for space-worthiness and was coming back?"

"Apparently, that bot he picked up begged him to stay for some reason."

Galina laughed. "That cleaning bot? I knew he had a soft spot for it. But what about Gregory? I thought he was helping Leon? Shouldn't he have the plating fixed by now with his help?"

Miles' camera turned towards Galina. "While he often assists Leon, by utilizing Gregory's abilities on the weapons, we have decreased the mission time by a large factor."

Galina leaned back in her chair and fought not to float off of it. "A large factor? What, no details?"

"As Deven and others have requested, such details when not needed, only serve the purpose of –as has been said to me– 'filling time'."

"Wasting time, I think is what we said."

Miles' iris contracted and expanded again. "I do not believe it is a waste. Therefore, that is your opinion, not mine."

Galina rolled her eyes. "You dumb bot I–"

Deven held up his hand. "Galina, Miles, that is enough. I know everyone is still on edge and I promised some R&R. But we must do this first. Afterwards, we will all have some downtime."

"But Deven, I do not need 'downtime'," Miles said.

"Perhaps you don't, but we certainly do. And to be honest, I wonder about you as well. You are more human than you care to admit."

"Perhaps," Miles said. Another screen adjacent to Deven's lit up with targeting information. "I have located two more targets, they will be in range in three minutes."

"Good, proceed." Deven floated out of his chair and headed towards the hatch.

"Where are you going?" Galina said.

"Aleshia is down in our cabin. While she is a very understanding woman, she is not happy we are up here and not in Bermuda like we planned."

"Yeah, don't want to make that girl mad, that is for sure." Galina grinned.

Deven chuckled. "I don't intend to." He floated off of the bridge and towards the cabins.

Want to find out what happens? Visit your favorite book store and pick up a copy of Silicon Strike! Available in both print and e-book editions.

About The Author

Don is the author of eight science fiction novels and many more short stories. He lives in the USA where he continues to dream up more fantastic worlds for you to enjoy. When not writing, he can usually be found devouring another science fiction book, TV series, or movie.

Other works by Don DeBon:

The Husband

Erin's Husband is not himself.

One night he returns from a walk in the woods a changed man. He walks like him, talks like him, yet is very different. No one believes her, leaving Erin alone to find out the truth. Truth that could have dire consequences for the entire human race. What happened that caused him to change so radically?

Red Warp

In a race against time the casualty could be your life.

If you could travel through time with just yourself and no machine needed, would you?

Meet Red, a woman with an amazing gift, the gift of passing though time and space without the need of any bulky equipment. The places she has seen, the people she has helped will blow your mind.

Now meet James, just your average newly minted FBI agent minding his own business until he is thrust headlong into Red's world. A world he didn't ask for, but one that hit him in the face full force. Can they get along long enough to survive?

Time Rock

Time Travel. Blessing or curse? One man thinks he has it all figured out but what began as a simple test has turned into a nightmare. With his equipment failing all around him, only Red and James can save him. Can they reach him in time?

Word of mouth is crucial for authors. If you enjoyed this book, would you consider leaving a review? It is very much appreciated.

Amazon USA
http://www.amazon.com/

Goodreads
http://www.goodreads.com

Connect with the Author
Email: writer.don.debon@gmail.com
Mailing List: http://eepurl.com/bxWAov
Website: http://www.dondebon.com
Twitter: @DonDeBon

This Edition Published 2022 by
DBDigital Publishing

ISBN 978-1-948819-12-1
ISBN 978-1-948819-08-4 **(e-book)**